PENGUIN YOUNG READERS LICENSES
An imprint of Penguin Random House LLC, New York

First published in Australia by Puffin Books, 2021

First published in the United States of America by Penguin Young Readers Licenses,
an imprint of Penguin Random House LLC, New York, 2022

This edition published as part of the *Bluey Outdoor Fun Box Set* by Penguin Young Readers Licenses,
an imprint of Penguin Random House LLC, New York, 2023

This book is based on the TV series *Bluey*.

Visit us online at penguinrandomhouse.com.

Manufactured in China

Box Set ISBN 9780593660836

10 9 8 7 6 5 4 3 2 HH

It's a hot summer's day, and Bluey wants to know what the family is going to do.

"Nothing, until you've cleaned your teeth," says Mum. But Bluey doesn't want to.

"**BORING** things are **IMPORTANT**, too," says Mum.

Bluey thinks that if boring things were important, then they'd be more **FUN**.

Dad bursts in.

"Let's go for a swim in Uncle Stripe's pool!" yells Dad.

"Yeah!" cry the girls.

"Don't forget the swim stuff," calls Mum. But Bluey, Bingo, and Dad are already rushing out the door and into the car.

"Mum is such a fusspot. She always makes us do **BORING** things," says Bluey.

"She does," says Dad.

When they get to Uncle Stripe's, Bluey leaps down onto the footpath. It's hot!

Bluey and Bingo don't have their sandals.

So Dad ends up carrying them.
I'm a GIRAFFE!

Then it's time for Bluey and Bingo to put on their rashies and sunscreen. But Dad's forgotten them.

"We'll just have to stay in the shady bit, and we'll put our hats on," says Dad.

"What hats?" asks Bluey.

Bluey does a cannonball into the pool.
This is going to be **FUN!**

Bingo wants to jump in, too.
"Dad, can I have my floaties?" she asks.

"Sorry, Squirt, I didn't bring them," says Dad.

Bingo's not sure about the crawly thing, either!

Bluey wants to swim all the way to the other end of the pool. But she can't go into the sunny bit.

"You've got no sunscreen on," reminds Dad.

"Dad, is the shady bit going to get **BIGGER** or **SMALLER?**"
asks Bluey.

"Ah . . . **BIGGER**, for sure," says Dad.

"I meant **smaller**," says Dad.

The pool doesn't seem
that much **FUN** anymore.

Dad, I'm bored.

Dad, I'm cold.

Dad, I'm freezing.

Dad, I'm hungry.

Dad, I'm starving.

DAD!

DAD!

DAD!

DAD!

DAD!

DAD!

"Okay. Can everyone stop saying 'Dad'!" says Dad.

"I think Dad is actually **BORING**. Mum is way more **FUN!**" declares Bluey.

A warm voice floats into the pool area.

"Oh, that's nice to hear," says Mum. "I brought all the swim stuff you left behind."

Mum even remembered to bring morning tea.

After they've eaten,
Mum helps Bluey put
on some sunscreen.

And Dad helps Bingo
with her floaties.

"So **BORING** things are **IMPORTANT** sometimes, then?" asks Mum.

"Yes!" agrees Bluey.

Goggles mean
Bluey can play
torpedo.

Floaties mean Bingo can
escape from the crawly thing.

And sinkies take you to the very bottom of the pool . . .

. . . where you can see all sorts of things.

PENGUIN YOUNG READERS LICENSES
An imprint of Penguin Random House LLC, New York

First published in Australia by Puffin Books, 2020

First published in the United States of America by Penguin Young Readers Licenses,
an imprint of Penguin Random House LLC, New York, 2020

This edition published as part of the *Bluey Outdoor Fun Box Set* by Penguin Young Readers Licenses,
an imprint of Penguin Random House LLC, New York, 2023

This book is based on the TV series *Bluey*.

Visit us online at penguinrandomhouse.com.

Manufactured in China

Box Set ISBN 9780593660836

10 9 8 7 6 5 4 3 2 HH

Bluey's bored of the playground.
She's played on everything twice.

Mackenzie has an idea.
"What about we go to
the creek?"

"Yeah, I'll take you down to the creek," says Dad.

"YAYYY!" cry the kids.

Dad scoops up Bingo and races off. "Let's bush bash!"

Bluey holds back. She's not sure what the creek is like. Maybe she might just stay in the playground . . .

But Mackenzie won't let her. "C'mon, Bluey!
THE CREEK IS BEAUTIFUL!"

The creek is very different
from the playground.

There are more thorns here.

More spiders . . .

. . . and **DEFINITELY** more leeches!

But there's also more of these fellas.

The gang heads down a slope. The ground is more uneven here. And there are no steps like at the playground!

"Wow," says Bingo when they arrive at the creek.
Both Mackenzie and Bingo think **THE CREEK IS BEAUTIFUL**.
But Bluey still wonders if they're right.

Dad and Bingo lead them to the spot where he played as a kid. They rock hop across the water.

Some of the rocks are pointy. Others are wobbly.

And the green ones are slippery!

"It's so lovely."

"THE CREEK IS BEAUTIFUL," Bluey says to herself.

"I'm not scared of it at all."
But she might be a little.

Bluey is getting the hang of the creek!

"You made it, Squirt!" says Dad.

The creek is an adventure.

"Here we are! I don't think I've been to the creek since I was your age," says Dad. "It still looks the same."

The creek must be really old then.

Bluey's not sure what to play. In the playground it is easy. But the creek is different.

Just then
a dragonfly
flutters past.

And Bluey just starts
mucking around.

Skipping stones . . .

. . . and making boats.

And building dams.

Bluey thinks the creek is fun.

At Daddy Day Spa, Dad finally gets his nails done.

Bingo slops a mud pack on Dad. "This will make you very beautiful. Oh, I'm out of mud!"

"I'll get some more," volunteers Bluey and heads off.

Bluey squelches her paws into the mud.
Suddenly, there's a rustling noise.
Bluey looks up and gasps.

A potoroo!

They stare at each other, the potoroo's nose twitching before it bounds off.

As the gang heads home,
Bluey doesn't have to wonder
if Mackenzie and Bingo were right.
She knows for sure,
deep inside . . .

. . . that **THE CREEK IS BEAUTIFUL**.

THE BEACH

PENGUIN YOUNG READERS LICENSES
An imprint of Penguin Random House LLC, New York

First published in Australia by Puffin Books, 2019

First published in the United States of America by Penguin Young Readers Licenses,
an imprint of Penguin Random House LLC, New York, 2021

This edition published as part of the *Bluey Outdoor Fun Box Set* by Penguin Young Readers Licenses,
an imprint of Penguin Random House LLC, New York, 2023

This book is based on the TV series *Bluey*.

Visit us online at penguinrandomhouse.com.

Manufactured in China

Box Set ISBN 9780593660836

10 9 8 7 6 5 4 3 2 HH

Bluey, Bingo, Mum, and Dad are off to the beach.

They set up the tent, roll around in the sand, and then race to the water.

Bluey and Bingo pretend the waves are trying to splash them.

Here comes a **BIG** one!

Mum is off for a walk along the beach.

"Why do you like walking by yourself?" asks Bluey.

"I'm not sure," says Mum. "**I JUST DO.** See you soon, little mermaid."

What a strange answer, thinks Bluey.

Not long after, she finds a beautiful shell and asks to show Mum.

"All right, off you go," says Dad.

"FOR REAL LIFE?" says Bluey. "All by myself?"

Dad nods. "Just don't go in the water."

Bingo waves her hands over Bluey's tail.
Bluey laughs. "I am the mermaid who got her **LEGS!**"

Mum is now a tiny orange speck.

"Hmmm." Bluey frowns. "Maybe I'll just stay here with you and Dad."

"But, little mermaid, you can follow Mum's footsteps," says Bingo.

"OH YEAH!" Bluey grins. "Thanks!"

Bluey **HOPS** from one footprint to another.
She **RUNS** and **SKIPS** and does **CARTWHEELS**
in the sand until . . .

. . . she comes across a flock of seagulls.

"Um, can you **please** move?" Bluey asks politely.

It's a good thing mermaids aren't scared of seagulls!

Bluey laughs as she **HOPS** from one footprint to another. She **RUNS** and **SKIPS** and does **CARTWHEELS** in the sand until . . .

. . . a **BIG** wave sneaks up and **CRASHES** onto the shore. It takes Mum's footsteps out to sea.

"Ooh, you **CHEEKY** wave!" Bluey barks. "How will I find Mum now?"

Just as Bluey begins to lose hope, she spots a pipi coming up for **wee-wees!**

A crab scuttles past.

Bluey copies its funny sideways walk.

"**Ha-Ha!** I am the mermaid who got her **CRAB LEGS!**"

Bluey scampers away.

. . . then **SKIDS** to a stop. "A jellyfish! How will I get past?"

She picks up a stick and
pokes the blue blob.
It wobbles hello.

"Ha-ha! You can't sting me, jellyfish!
I am the mermaid who got her legs, but only for a day!"

Bluey races ahead.

"Look at this amazing shell!" she calls, but Mum's still too far away to hear.

Better keep going!

Bluey **RUNS** and **SKIPS** and does **CARTWHEELS** in the sand until she comes across an old castle.

Perhaps this is where all the other mermaids lived, she thinks, and leaves her stick as a present.

Then she slowly backs away and bumps right into . . .

. . . a pelican!

Bluey begins to think she's had enough of walking by herself . . .

She looks back at Dad, but he's just a tiny blue speck.

"If I can't go backwards, and I can't go forwards, what am I going to do?"

Bluey remembers the seagulls and the crabs and the jellyfish. If she got past them, maybe she can get past a pelican, too . . .

She summons every bit of courage. After all, a little mermaid has got to be brave.

Then she tiptoes around the pelican.

The pelican beats his great big wings and flies away.

THANK YOU FOR MOVING, MR. PELICAN!

A familiar voice floats towards Bluey.
She gasps and spins around.

Bluey holds the shell to Mum's ear. It has the whole beach inside it.

Bluey and Mum head back together.

"I **LOVE** walking by myself," says Bluey.

"Oh yeah, why's that?" asks Mum.

Bluey thinks. That's a hard question. "I don't know, **I JUST DO**."

BLUEY

CAMPING

PENGUIN YOUNG READERS LICENSES
An imprint of Penguin Random House LLC, New York

First published in Australia by Puffin Books, 2020

First published in the United States of America by Penguin Young Readers Licenses,
an imprint of Penguin Random House LLC, New York, 2022

This edition published as part of the *Bluey Outdoor Fun Box Set* by Penguin Young Readers Licenses,
an imprint of Penguin Random House LLC, New York, 2023

This book is based on the TV series *Bluey*.

Visit us online at penguinrandomhouse.com.

Manufactured in China

Box Set ISBN 9780593660836

10 9 8 7 6 5 4 3 2 HH

The Heelers are on a camping trip. Bluey wants to build a stick house with Bingo, but Mum has other plans.

"Bingo's coming with me," Mum says. "She hasn't had a bath in **THREE DAYS!**"

So, off Bluey goes to the creek, alone.

As Bluey searches for sticks, she hears a voice.

"Bonjour."

"Hi! My name's Bluey."

"*Salut*, Bluey. *Je suis* Jean Luc."

Bluey doesn't understand what Jean Luc is saying, but that doesn't stop them building a stick house together.

OH! C'EST TRÈS BEAU.

"Now we need some food to eat," says Bluey.

"We can plant this seed, like farmers! This will grow into a big tree with fruit on it."

"But it might take a while," she adds. "And we need something to eat *now*."

Suddenly, they hear a **HOWL** coming through the forest.

"HIDE!" shouts Bluey.

"It's a wild pig," Bluey says.

"Sanglier!" says Jean Luc.

Bluey and Jean Luc make a plan to capture the wild pig, but . . .

. . . he escapes!

Never mind.

"Bluey, dinner!"
Mum calls.

Then Jean Luc's
dad calls to him,
"Jean Luc, *dîner*!"

"See you tomorrow!"
Bluey says.

They both run off
to their families.

GOOD NIGHT.

BONNE NUIT.

The next morning, Bluey and Jean Luc are ready to play.

"Hmm, no fruit tree yet. We need a better plan to catch that wild pig, or we will have no food for the winter!"

"I've got an idea," Bluey tells Jean Luc.
"My dad taught me how to do this."

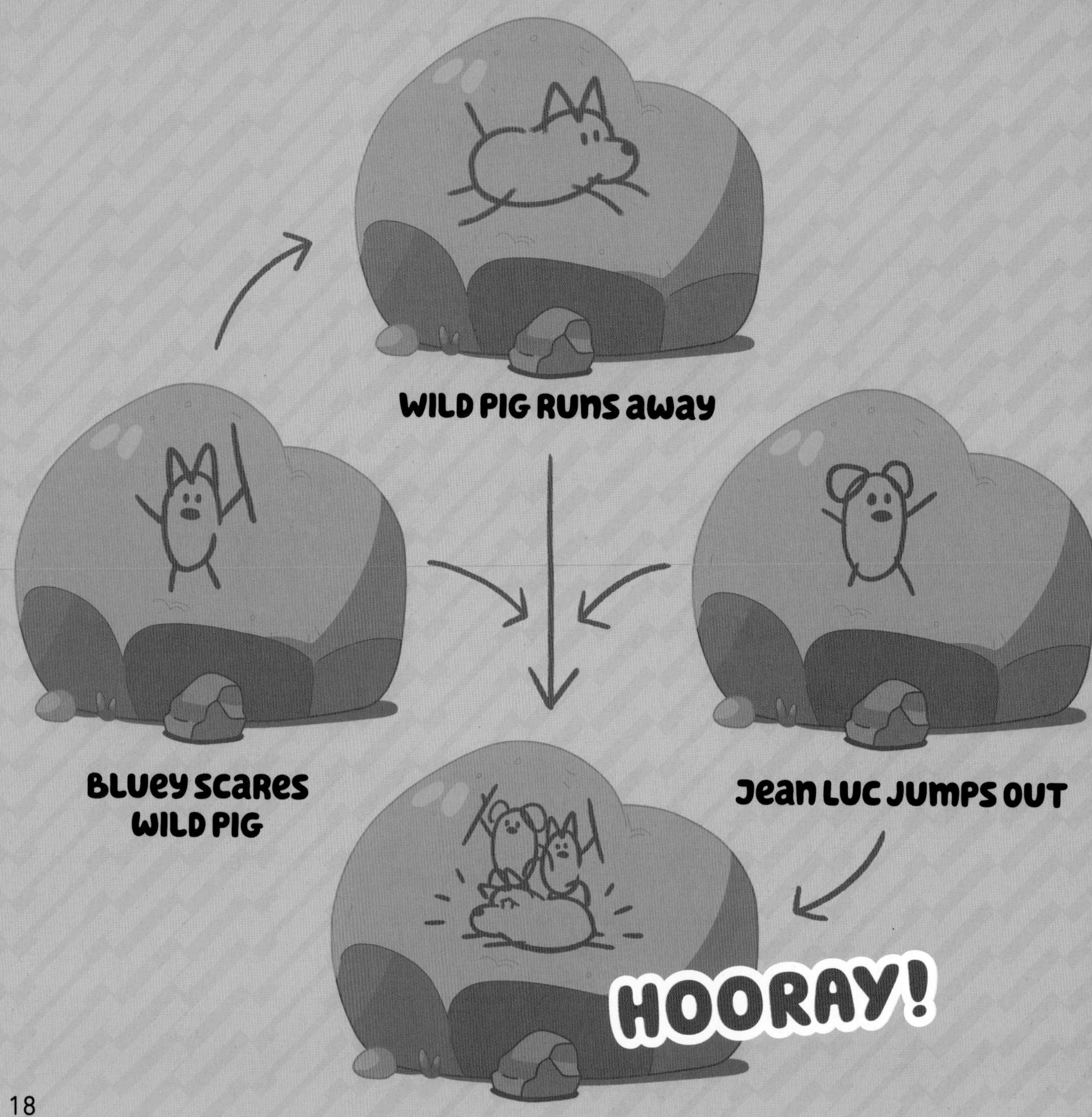
WILD PIG RUNS away
BLUey SCares WILD PIG
Jean LUC JUMPS OUT
HOORAY!

They wait until they hear the wild pig **ROAR**, and then . . .

YARRRR!

It's time to head back to camp for the night.

"Goodbye, Jean Luc," says Bluey happily. "See you tomorrow."

"*Non*, Bluey," Jean Luc calls.

"*Au revoir!*"

The next morning, Bluey discovers that the seed they planted is growing into a little tree.

But she can't see Jean Luc anywhere. Not at his campsite . . .

. . . or at their stick house.

Bluey runs back to Mum, who tells her that Jean Luc must have left. His holiday is over.

"What?!" says Bluey. "You mean they're gone?"

"I'm afraid so, sweetheart."

That night, while Bingo has a bush wee,
Bluey asks Mum why Jean Luc had to leave.

“Sometimes special people come into our lives, stay for a bit, and then they have to go,” says Mum.

"But that's sad," says Bluey.

"It is," says Mum. "But the bit where they were here was happy, wasn't it?"

"Yeah. We caught a wild pig together!" Bluey says.

"Maybe that makes it all worth it," says Mum.

"Will I ever see him again?" asks Bluey.

"Well, you never know," says Mum.

"The world's a magical place."
"Hello, Bluey."